Hello, Family Members,

Learning to read is one of the most important accomplishments of early childhood. **Hello Reader!** books are designed to help children become skilled readers who like to read. Beginning readers learn to read by remembering frequently used words like "the," "is," and "and"; by using phonics skills to decode new words; and by interpreting picture and text clues. These books provide both the stories children enjoy and the structure they need to read fluently and independently. Here are suggestions for helping your child *before*, *during*, and *after* reading:

Before

- Look at the cover and pictures and have your child predict what the story is about.
- Read the story to your child.
- Encourage your child to chime in with familiar words and phrases.
- Echo read with your child by reading a line first and having your child read it after you do.

During

- Have your child think about a word he or she does not recognize right away. Provide hints such as "Let's see if we know the sounds" and "Have we read other words like this one?"
- Encourage your child to use phonics skills to sound out new words.
- Provide the word for your child when more assistance is needed so that he or she does not struggle and the experience of reading with you is a positive one.
- Encourage your child to have fun by reading with a lot of expression . . . like an actor!

After

- Have your child keep lists of interesting and favorite words.
- Encourage your child to read the books over and over again. Have him or her read to brothers, sisters, grandparents, and even teddy bears. Repeated readings develop confidence in young readers.
- Talk about the stories. Ask and answer questions. Share ideas about the funniest and most interesting characters and events in the stories.

I do hope that you and your child enjoy this book.

—Francie Alexander
Reading Specialist,
Scholastic's Learning Ventures

To The Haldane School Foundation
— J. Marzollo

For my husband, Bill:
You rock my world
— J. Moffatt

Go to www.scholastic.com for Web site information
on Scholastic authors and illustrators.

Library of Congress Cataloging-in-Publication Data

Marzollo, Jean
    I am planet earth / by Jean Marzollo; illustrated by Judith Moffatt.
        p. cm. —(Hello reader! science — Level 1)
    Summary: The planet Earth describes its location in the solar system, its atmosphere, geographic features, and treatment by the people who live on it.
    ISBN 0-439-11321-0 (pbk.)
    1. Earth Juvenile literature. [1. Earth.] I. Moffatt, Judith, ill. II. Title.
III. Series
QB631.4.M37 2001
525—dc21

                                      99-15529
                                         CIP

10 9 8 7 6   01 02 03 04 05 06

Printed in the U.S.A. 24
First printing, March 2001

I Am Planet Earth

by Jean Marzollo
Illustrated by Judith Moffatt

Hello Reader! Science—Level 1

SCHOLASTIC INC. Cartwheel ·B·O·O·K·S·®
New York   Toronto   London   Auckland   Sydney
Mexico City   New Delhi   Hong Kong

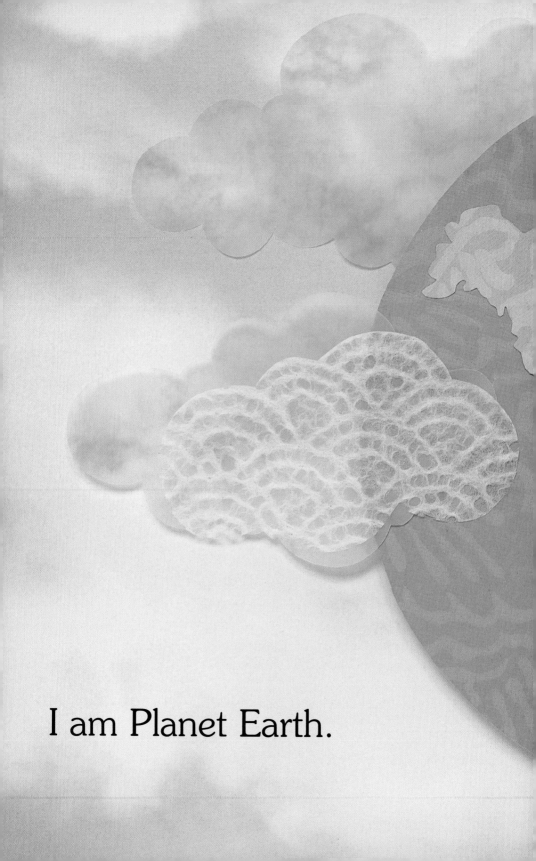

I am Planet Earth.

EARTH

I am the third planet
from the sun.
The sun gives me
heat and light.

I have many fine things.
I have cool, wet water.

I have hot, dry sand.

I have leafy trees
and jungles.

I have mountains and valleys.

I have warm, green
rice paddies.

I have cold, white ice.

I have animals.

I have people.

I have towns.

I have cities.

And I have you.
Can you find where you live?

Can you find where you were born?

Pretend a light
is the sun.
Shine the light
on the globe.
Can you see how the sun
makes night and day?

Night and day,
I am your planet,
the only one you have.
Please, take care of me.